"Hold fast to dreams, for if dreams die,
life is a broken-winged bird that cannot fly."

- Langston Hughes

Also by Fabrice Poussin

In Absentia, (Silver Bow Publishing 2021)
If I Had a Gun, (Silver Bow Publishing 2022)
Half Past Life (Silver Bow Publishing 2023)
The Temptation of Silence (Silver Bow Publishing 2024)

Forgive Me
For
Dreaming

Fabrice Poussin

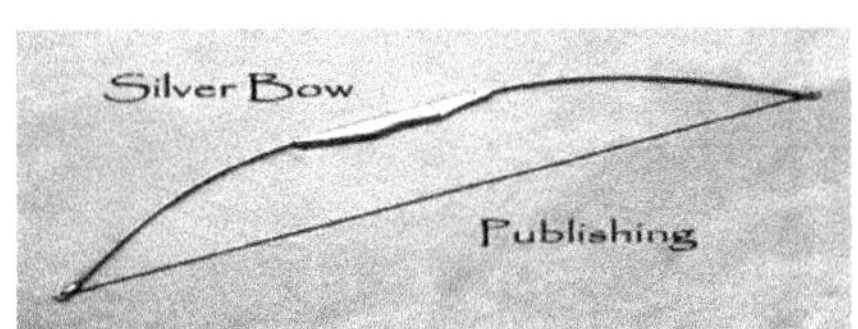

720 Sixth Street, Unit #5
New Westminster, BC
V3L 3C5
CANADA

Title: Forgive Me for Dreaming
Author: Fabrice Poussin
Publisher: Silver Bow Publishing
Cover Art: photo by Fabrice Poussin
Cover Layout and Design: Candice James

www.silverbowpublishing.com
info@silverbowpublishing.com
ISBN: 978-1-77403- 373-9 paperback
ISBN: 978-1-77403- 374-6 electronic book

Library and Archives Canada Cataloguing in Publication

Library and Archives Canada Cataloguing in Publication

Title: Forgive me for dreaming / Fabrice Poussin.
Other titles: Forgive me for dreaming (Compilation)
Names: Poussin, Fabrice, author.
Identifiers: Canadiana (print) 20250219530 | Canadiana (ebook) 20250220946 | ISBN 9781774033739
   (softcover) | ISBN 9781774033746 (Kindle)
Subjects: LCGFT: Poetry.
Classification: LCC PS3616.O875 F67 2025 | DDC 811/.6—dc23

"To the students who always encourage me
to discover new authors."

Contents

Calories

The epidemic of the millennia ambles to the grave
as if a nasty surprise at the end of the buffet line
so few seem concerned that they shift shapes
overnight before once more heading for another
grease spot, mecca of sugar-coated ailments.

Tastes of heaven trick their senses
with aromas from below, sights never before seen
dripping, oozing like caramel on a mountain
topped with a cream whipped a hundred-fold
while heavy chocolate timidly hides to better strike.

Humanoids march in perfect order by the full-size
mirror; do they fail to notice the reflection
their ten-year-old self may not have recognized
when they walked into that strange hall of
comical horrors at the county fair.

Roundness follows in every locale
bolstering incomprehensible sounds
pride of not going unnoticed whatever the cost
while hearts struggle to complete their task
suffocating under the weight of colossus.

It is an eerie army outfitted in a new fashion
sizes in quadruples and growing still
they model the skirts, dresses, and pantaloons
to the charmed glances of their kin,
compliments made up in darkness.

Age of Silence

Four they come, girls and boys
perhaps on the dates they dreamed of;
they, blond, and slender with carefree eyes
the others, tall, ready for another big game.

Welcome by the familiar voice,
they know what they need to bear smiles
mixtures of sweets, beans, and crème
they have little time for words.

It will be a minute or two before it is done
these hot delights ready for their glee
they must wait for life to come forward
fill the eternal seconds with meaning.

The faux leather seats swallow them eager
as they collapse without a sound
adjusting their touch to the glossy screens
it is time to scroll mindless pages by the hundreds.

And now silence between the guests
intimate strangers who share a ride
to the store, unconscious through life
they might dissolve before our very eyes.

Just Like 1984

This year soon to end
will die and be forgotten
given next to the hands of madmen
greedy only for the power they may grasp
while the ignorant bystanders die.

Many decades old and still trying to achieve
the dream of a father long gone
danger to the innocent children
who only hope for restful days
while the skies become heavier.

No more truth unless it is what he decrees
the gross oddity trying to found a dynasty
on empty brains and great cruelty
so he may fill his pockets with gold
and watch them all die without a hiccup.

Followed by his groupies he has made an army
of Satans who surround their master
like minor devils eager to please a giant
although the stench of his rottenness
permeates through the whole land.

Too afraid of what is real he forces everyone
to silence unless they can speak like him
and pretend nothing before him is true
for, you see, he thinks of himself as no less
than a God, this Big Brother of century-old Wax.

Backstage

Hallways are narrow
props abound against the walls
a dress code officer runs
stumbles to an unfound
finish line.

In the prescribed darkness
a TV monitor tells the story
unraveling on the nearby stage
singing, laughing; strange silhouettes
dance by subdued multicolored lights.

Some wait their turn to the crowd
patiently nervous in this great chaos,
lines collide in their eager souls;
will they recall every little move
smile, giggle, gesture?

A prop master desperately seeks
fake cigars, a bottle of bourbon filled
with a taste of Southern iced tea
while a smothered crash signals
the almost missed discovery.

Hours will turn into two different worlds
nothing too real but what lies out of doors
frantic silhouettes deliver upon order
to those who declaim a temporary
universe to them in search of catharsis.

Rarely do they freeze in their steps;
there is no room for error in their world
of magicians until the final curtain
when all bow and get the well-earned
ovation and a new sun rises yet again.

Tomorrow they will awaken and begin
a new adventure while contemplating
the empty box where they all became other,
puzzled, saddened, voided of these personas
they created, if for a brief fortnight.

Broken Lamp

There is a crowd growing near the fire hydrant
strangers in search of Sunday gossip
whispering questions with pre-made replies.

Someone heard a commotion a little after 6 PM
Eagerly hoping for a tale to emerge in this neighborhood
sleepy, but for those precious moments.

The air had been thick with thunder for hours;
few dared to venture on the burning grounds
waiting as they often do, to burst into an end.

Still, the flame came too close to the powder room
pushed as it was from hostile dominions
it exploded as the door slammed onto a forgotten peace.

An eternity for the ones who fell to the unexpected hatred
too brief a spectacle for witnesses who long to live
vicarious lives and tales of horror only others know.

They ponder as the sirens crash through the air
whether at last tragedy will enlighten their years
craning necks worthy of terrifying undertakers.

Concerned gazes mean little to people in flip-flops
while numerous broods chase others with water hoses
unless the morning paper has a bloody front page.

Behind brick walls the lovers cry once again
exhausted by a quarrel they do not understand
collapsed on a wrinkly couch, they slowly breathe.

Ignorant of the petty groups outside
they contemplate the ancient lamp by the hearth
broken as it was the week before.

The police will ring, and all will be fine
next week they will go to the lake house
to embrace in a world made just for them.

Curtain

The lights went out
we sang our last line
we bowed to the invisibles
rushed to the dressing room
a few laughs, quick recall
of missed cues, improved mishaps;
it was time to drop the airs.

The ambassador took to the street
encountering strangers at a fast pace
while they stumbled, a little dizzy
with the night's drink and excitement
torn-up jeans and a branded T;
no one recognized in him
the gesture of a whimsical hour.

No sadness in his gait; a fact of life
the show is done and must not go on
another re-creation will be hidden in the wardrobe
an army of soldiers never to see the light again
albeit perhaps under different skies;
times long forgotten of wars never fought.

A little teary, the diplomat is no more
in the slick hybrid he drives on
the interstate deserted at the late hour
wide-eyed in search of his next venture
a paycheck to last perhaps a fortnight
a meal, a roof, and temporary friends
for dreams made true for a lifetime.

Forgive Me For Dreaming

She looks away when he dreams of roses
her soul floating in a forceful prison
a smile made for ephemeral convenience.

Fidgeting into another moment she craves
an intruder to empower her solitude
insides curled, to a jealous safe house.

He moves to the gentle cover of heaven
in an instant frigid as if in the presence
of loathsome danger in the shape of a familiar stranger

Hiding again inside the false security
of an alcove so private it may be
in another dimension of this earthly realm.

Forgive me for dreaming when you close
your door to the eternal gift made
of the infinite bond of creation.

Fried Chicken and H2O

She walks at an impressive clip
across the lawn to prevent tardiness
a gallon jug in one hand
a bag filled with knowledge in the other.

Water is her religion in the early light
before the lectern of the master
as she delights in her streamlined munches
a lunch made perhaps for a robin or a sparrow.

I admire the resolve of the late teens' girl
to hold on to a great regimen of health
strength training and many, many steps
through the pure air of country paths.

Yet mid-morning comes upon a snack
of deep-fried chicken, sweet tea and
a Grande Frappuccino so she may
keep these browns wide-eyed for another minute.

A little later, past two, time to explore
the bountiful options of the vending machine
nachos, sweets, and of course a diet drink
for, you see, lunch is still two hours until dark.

Now she needs another pick me up
to study, play, perhaps even party a little
before bedtime at two. Pizza thrown in
a hurry to a microwave, and another sweet cola.

Ah! How good it feels to amble the halls
with a gallon of H2O, and a few thoughts
for a better physique so long as all this
is balanced by the heavy weight of sweets.

Girl in the Green Skirt

No one knows how to pronounce her name
in any language other than her own;
I saw her with saddest tears and reddened cheeks
as we parted ways perhaps forever.

Obliged to wear the fateful mask of the
early 20's, nothing stopped her from partaking
in the daily adventures of her little group
even when her voice failed her.

Sequestered for the sake of the universe
we were told we might not celebrate her presence
every day as we wished but she
proved them wrong and spoke until time was gone.

Grief

A black hole as I have read about often
gaping before me, reminds of jolly times
when most things were bright and full
of color.

But something suddenly changed
with a long-distance call and
a quick turnaround as I too have
so often made.

It was time I suppose for me to know
the void one leaves behind upon parting
unsuspecting of the hurt they may cause.

It is now December every day
August freezes in the balmy evenings
and I am all out of tears.

I stare at the trunk full of memories
anxious for glorious tomorrows
but it is now locked for good.

Within, a soul remains imprisoned
victim of its own shortcomings
shy to a fault, terrified to speak the truth.

Soon it may tilt into the abyss
and fall for eternity in echoing distress
unable to hold onto what
could have been.

Half-Broken Old Granny

A short distance to the ancestral home
memories of a medieval fortress
she walked half-broken, the old granny.

Walking stick to the ground, eyes on the prize
for a quick chat with a son
and the new kin he gave her.

Bones soon to dust she could still laugh
after a little snuff and dark coffee,
she sought news of the kingdom.

Half-broken the old granny, always a feast
to see her as she braved hot and cold
to greet us with a well-tried voice.

Decades have passed and I am still not sure
of your first name; just vague remembrances
of this little girl once adopted, I was told.

Almost half a century since you escaped
the old carcass, prison no longer strong enough
to hold you captive.

Now you walk straight in the land of dreams.

Holiday Shopping

Four cases of light beer in aluminum cans
two packs of Marlboro reds
the lady pushes the buggy to the rusty
old minivan where the kids await.

The face of this ex-twenty-something
adorned with too many premature lines
betrayed by a voice raspy with drought
as if she had been lost in the Mohave for a lifetime.

She smiles as she struggles to find the plastic
that will again allow her to purchase
what she cannot afford and should not privilege
over the goods a gentle body may prefer.

It is another late November for her
a repeat of other months of feasting
May, July, September, and many other excuses
found to ignore a peace that matters more.

What may she do with the cheap brew
and those cancer sticks so unpopular,
another Thanksgiving celebrated before
it's too late for her to see the next?

We all recall her handsome figure well
as she dictated the fashion of the week
a tiny bikini under hottest suns or perhaps
a coat made of fur for winter eves.

Her skin quasi-mummified, she walks yet;
for how long will the masquerade continue
as she visits the local alcohol and tobacco stores
her heart forcing for a halt as it flutters into the dark?

Interstates

There is great excitement at the thought
of undertaking that journey across the land
from ocean to ocean, through mountains
vales, deserts, and broad rivers.

So much to contemplate for children of all ages
singing oldies, listening to the classics
telling endless stories of first times
when life was not so different after all.

They point to wonders on all sides of the road
colorful plates from states and other lands;
debris litters shoulders abandoned of the workers
who once labored to create these great paths.

But who are those strangers we meet?
They might go West, North, East to a realm
were their dreams are yet to be made,
in such a hurry as they haul their treasures.

There a Tesla, here a Mustang, followed by a semi
an old rusty truck that has seen the world
a minivan on its last wheel, and a beautiful home
longer than a bus, worth the earning of a lifetime.

So many lives we will not see again
as we cross Big Muddy, the Rockies, and Death Valley,
CEOS in a rush to their next meetings,
plumbers, thieves, perhaps even dealers in illicit powders.

There may be a star or two resting in a limo
before their next interview with Oprah;
but we keep driving eighty to be polite,
unknown too, happy owners of priceless fancies.

Last Walk

I saw him sublime into the distance
on a native river path so long gone;
those miles he knew well for many years,
too will vanish as if they never were.

Sharing in the stories he read
often alone at dusk and dawn
he did not see the few who dared
disturb the peace he so dearly sought.

Communing with the trees and their critter friends
his eyes transfixed by the fires in the sky
he counted the steps into the hourglass
aware he was entering another realm.

I wonder if perhaps eternity will carry
the trace he made so faithfully,
glad in the undisturbed days he made
as autumn leaves made a cocoon for him.

Lawnmowers, Leaf Blowers,
and Weed Whackers, Oh My!

Saturday in early spring
perhaps evening too
the same sounds borne to
neighborhoods limitless.

A cacophony of well-known sounds;
these men love the raucous they
can still organize, weapon in hand
to fight the green enemy.

Fueled with old fossils, new energy
and a great amount of elbow grease
mowers, whackers, and blowers on every corner
every street, disrupt the gentle monotony.

Determined, beer in hand, cigarette glued to the lips
they wave at the others, their clones
chests bare dripping with pearly sweat
skin reddened by too much sun.

Celebration of the old boys now
masters of their own houses, commanders in chief
fingers on the magic button they pray
for a symphony of roaring sounds.

They cut, they whack, and they blow
full of the delicious aromas of a new summer
it is a life of leisure. well-earned at the cost of
decades and a little freedom.

Le Tourneau's Penny

I hear the train's loud rumble
memories of days in the sun
western Texas and its undefinable
steel roads through oil fields
with an invisible horizon
almost nothing out of sight.

He flashed a friendly smile
through an uneven row of brownish teeth
a half cigarette stuck to dried lips
plagues with blisters as if perhaps
he lived in the Northern lands
between the Pole and the Yukon.

He liked to claim he hailed from the East
proud owner of a degree from Letourneau
the name he went by out of habit
now he lived on the roads hopping
from train to train to nowhere for
so long as there was no end,
there was hope, he said.

He enjoyed flipping that shiny coin upon a talk
a copper penny, his only treasure
possession of a childhood so long gone
when he rode the rusty bike,
and a few scratches
the same laughter his only trademark
into a present with no worries,
no need for hope.

My eyes are heavy with the news
a grainy old sepia on page fifteen
a man without a name, but a great grin
collided with the metal beast in the night
no one knew his name, but I,
at the mention of his beloved copper coin.

Just Like He Said

Will you please listen for a moment
dear unknown of few meaningless words
bathed in so many likes and let's pretend
acquiescence in the shape of "Yeahs!"

It takes more than a nod and a word
to communicate love in the wild
when I am looking for meaning in you
but you hear only the sounds you repeat.

I wonder what you have learned
in the hours with the old man
and agreed with all he said
a smile here, a giggle there.

He may have tired of your endless sighs
and exhaled a deep breath when at last
he remembered he had a place to be,
quiet, remote, one hundred miles away.

I must say, we have never met
as I look to my left for rest
in the eyes of the silent girl
dreaming in the deep of her eyes.

Little Black Dress

Fits like a glove in summer
enveloping sharp tan lines
the dress abandoned so long
for these cruel winter eves.

Gifted with its own persona it seems
to saunter with unsuspected grace
determined to the end of the path
dark to the endless journey.

Gently following the curves
the soft fabric tells many stories of
a childhood so long forgotten
yet still fresh with every step she takes.

Barely a sound follows her
so glad she remains to glide
through life, seen but untouchable
alive somewhere between two worlds.

Like a statuesque girl of true flesh
she may have been sculpted in ancient days
victorious Athena, glorious Aphrodite
through the black garment, she transcends eternity.

Memories

Ten years old and a love letter
in hand to share in a sweet bounty
to discover that the adults knew
and spread the news to the village.

One year more and a new interest
most beautiful of those who rode the bus
daughter of a most famous man
in a thousand the only bread maker.

Little time passes that feels like eternities
another grade, she walks in, carefree,
her dress made for the woman
she will be perhaps a little too soon.

Days of middle school quickly merge
on the threshold of less pleasant days
when little girls giggled without inhibitions
hearts healed as when they played spin the bottle.

Mr. Tough Guy

Hey, Mr. Loudmouth with all the horses
loud as so many tanks under a metal cover
why don't you cool your jets and see the light
so red, perhaps then you will know you are not
the number one who believes he has all the rights.

Hey, Mr. Big Guy with the bulging entrails
you walk as you may have been a duck once
marks of grease trace two weeks of your history
devouring fast food as you hurry down the road
screaming obscenities at those who smile at the forest.

Hey, Mr. Tough Guy, how was your day
why don't you smile behind the hair
take your foot off the gas, your tongue off the hate
pull over when there is still time for you
to have a life and dream while you sleep?

My Little life

My little life. That silly thing I
carry with me without so much
as a thought. It isn't worth a lot
don't you know?!

My little life and I we get along for
the most part. Yet we do wonder
sometimes. Why the two of us
keep going on the lonely road?

This little life. I look at it often and
ponder. Why is it of no interest to
anyone. It is after all the size of
others that pass by each day.

Won't you, little girl, be my friend and
cuddle this heart to make it warm.
you see, it was made just for you to hold
and nurture lest it may merely cease to be.

Odd Couple

5 AM, darkness blankets the trail
snaking through a semi-urban realm
even wildlife hesitates to venture
onto the uncertain surface.

Two silhouettes appear
same time, same place, every day
lovers, they might hold hands
but they may be ghosts.

Not a sound precedes them as they
continue along the curves
between the trees, silent,
they may be strangers.

Side by side, he, the bearded one
she, almost faceless
they utter not a word to the other
eerie figures never seen in the light.

Their encounter feels a threat
as the poet seeks inspiration
in a locale where no one else walks
but those in limbo in search of eternity.

One Snapshot at a Time

A rare color image of the ten-year-old
at a dinner party his parents made,
gleeful as he enjoyed the encounter
with a cousin, favorite playmate.

In black and white, he seemed a sad
toddler at the County Fair,
his gaze on the 120-film camera
a mother so hopeful for him.

He played into the future
alone in a cherry tree gorging
on the luscious fruit of summer
a relative laughed at his silliness.

A sister in trouble, too glad to help
he smiles at his success in the mud
her little Ford on a rainy day
a T adorned with new designs.

Lost in the crowd of a medieval celebration
she held the inexpensive box;
art available to the masses;
bad actor in a strange enactment, he smiled.

The old photo album closes
inanimate object with its own soul,
and he drifts into his preferred realm
dreams of a reality where she holds him dear.

Packing

It all began some time ago
long before she purchased a brand-new bag;
the little girl with the hot temper
tight shorts and all the right moves.

For years, she had an eye on the road;
gentle hands, painting nails in bright vermillion
a smile that sang many ironic tunes
slender legs made for an infinite future.

Her hair changed color again
perhaps it was the limelight on a beloved stage
as she twirled between her mates in
a light dress floating as if made of mist.

She may remain silent in her room
eager to feel the embrace of another hug
warm in the planned darkness of her bed
she dreams of the next day.

Her bags have been packed
last to leave the haven, already the walls echo
with the absence of two handsome ladies
no longer so little as both laugh in the distance.

Panic Room

It has no walls, this grand room of mine;
many endlessly soil its pathways
oblivious to the times marked there
solely for me on all the trees.

There is no electricity in this dark world
just a dim light, reflection of a lost star
and the symphonies made in heaven
when silence prevailed upon everything.

No borders either on the vast expanse
but the horizon infinite before and behind
where men attempt a great impression
of the lives they imagine are theirs.

It is not necessary to hide within concrete
and steel, and to breathe reprocessed air
to find refuge from all the madness;
a panic room wide open to the earth's bliss.

Perhaps a Bus Stop

They say hello in a rush
on their way to the restrooms
perfumed of freshness and bleach
not even time for a true smile.

They sit in the lounge, a book
in hand thick as an encyclopedia
nodding to the passerby as he walks
to search for a seat near the aisles.

One continues tapping her smartphone
for an urgent alert or a way to avoid
the love that could be laid over her;
this is only an hour in her week you know.

The giant screen streams from another room
aromas of fresh baked goods and dark brew;
I expect the next announcement to a gate,
my next journey to another city.

I forgot for a moment that this is a place
of worship where they are called to be
brothers and sisters in love, not
the lobby of international arrivals.

So Real When You Cry

You have lost a little in stature as
you take another step into the mist
thin of a late September day.

The shell of your daily attire screams
the well-defined beauty you carry
through my dreams.

Now you frown to avoid another tear
trapped deep in your soul
child of middle age hurting as an infant.

I stand back watching your heavy gait
so burdensome to bear as the distance
grows once again into the morning.

The hours have attacked with mighty blows
the caring heart opened to the vultures
in suits of navy ties adorned with fleur de lys.

I stand back and weep for you, the giantess
with your voice of wisdom carved onto
a melodious sheet a la Chopin.

She never shies from role
even when it sheds her very skin
for then, I offer her the safety of my world.

Coffee Shop Interviews

The characters in the novel raise eyebrows
interrupted in their lives by those loud visitors
casual, in jeans and worn-out shirts
they boast tattoos and speak of their
favorite baseball teams.

They are not looking for executive jobs
loaded with confused propositions;
they hope to make a living for now
speaking to the first newcomer, informal
salesperson from the bed of a pick-up.

They spend five minutes talking to the walls;
requests, expectations, and a few questions;
but they already knew, out of desperation
they might as well start to work
out of the liftgate of the rusty minivan.

Everyday a different trio, the same queries
like watching a rerun of a silly sitcom
late when no one follows the plot any longer;
no signature, no contract, just a handshake
and they part strangers, minutes into partners.

It is like all those corporate meetings;
managers talk, employees respond, distracted;
all walk away from the donuts and old waters
checking that other box on a busy schedule;
well done they say, and the world goes round in a wobble.

Stone of Bone

Stone on stone on bone,
cold and warm and new.
Home.

Eyes to the Heavens,
army hat on chest.
Asleep.

Holding on tight,
to his beautiful America.
Safe.

Dreaming of flowers,
sealed to words above.
Pleased.

A spec in immensity,
surrounded by stars.
Found.

Like the hand of God,
a quarter score has passed.
Touching.

Eyes meeting again,
lips longing for the kiss.
Finally.

Distance abolished,
time now irrelevant.
Forever.

Together again undeniably,
as one and all present.
Feeling.

In an endless embrace,
Of a billion galaxies.
Embracing.

Taj Mahal

Another frame to Taj Mahal
his eyes resting on the festive mist
contemplating a sunrise everyone knows.

Expert of all these sites, Far East
monuments which today and again
scream of him with their deep tones.

Strangers in foreign lands reflect his gaze;
no common tongue between them
they only share humanity from afar.

Then the canine with a deep blue stare
smiles at its friend of the last caress
steady, telling all of a life that is no more.

Store of Convenience

Tears must be shed when
the larger store of retail
adds that special aisle for
those who want the world
for a small fee.

Upon a little promenade
his Nobel freshly earned
still nimble the aging doctor
of astrophysics ponders yet
mysteries sealed in eternity.

Puzzled by the failing wheels
of an antiquated shopping cart
he raises his gaze to the deep blue sign
knowing he must enter this citadel
of infinite pseudo truths.

Before him a long queue of
baseball caps facing back
tattoos galore and greasy shirts
they seek their best bet, short of
the state jackpot.

The old man with his casual elegance
follows this group to the permanent
black Friday section of gift boxes
in shiny colors they all promise advanced degrees,
seven-figure pay, early retreat to a private island.

Not a spectacle for the philosophers of old
a scene of absolute greed
deprived of knowledge or intelligence
they get what they want with a wide grin
to benefit no one but fattening bellies

Meanwhile Mr. Nobel stands;
he might be trampled by ignorance
with Einstein, Marie Curie, and Papa,
his dream survives in old Sweden
but for how long… he sighs.

The Confession I Might Never Make

1832 I recall quite well
during a venture in the desolate park
I came upon an unexpected vision
of a man who seemed as wax.

Sitting in his great coat and high hat
I approached him with interest
for the story I may not have heard
if only he might still flow with life.

As I joined and greeted him simply
he raised his head to me with a meek smile;
he never thought anyone would so care
to spend a moment in his company.

He revealed that he had everything
others dreamed of under the faint stars
yet could no longer find his way to his home
a castle made of ice in summer months.

But his alcove remained frigid
in endless days of dark loneliness
as he stared at her from a distance
and knew not how to give her the truth.

Fearful that she may continue on her errands
smiling at so many passers-by in the wild city
he dared not take a place on his knees
and offer her his heart or the gold he owned.

I left him with a perfect portrait of her
that I may recognize upon a meeting
every curve with smiles and long black hair
highlighted by the azure of her eyes.

I do not know how long he remained there
for it was another era, another dream;
but I look to the heavens daily and hope
that he finally made his date with her in paradise.

The Days of Medicine

Quietly sitting on the night table
keenly centered in their orange bottles
recycled plastic and white tops
with a direction-laden label.

It is late into the dark and
the sleeper dreams like a rock
chest slowly heaving with a loud snore
the partner undisturbed by the familiar sound.

She fills each little section carefully
one for each day of the week of course
a few others for the more frequent
requirements of bones so old they weep.

It is a luxurious breakfast against the orders
of an expert in matters of life and death
for those who count their days
as another gift they never expected.

Watching his usual game shows at midday
he eyes the glass half-filled ready for the next
installment, a guarantee of a few more dawns
perhaps weeks or miraculous months.

Her face is drawn, wrinkles carved by the flames
of a fire burning too hot in the hearth
she sees her past dancing a little blurry
as she swallows the killer of torture.

Gone are the pain-free, drug-free days of their youth
if their eyes are sad, their souls unite yet
so they may escape for now into the home
they made for an eternal future.

The Hobo and the Snake

He looked down into the swollen river
in awe of the happening below
a rusty bicycle next to the trusted axe
made with rugged wood and duct tape.

He clearly was seeking companionship
if only for a moment before he sunk again
behind the thick wall of bushes and trees
so excited he was about the passing snake.

Others slowed their steps as well
as he nabbed them with his loud sounds
claiming a sight so rarely seen
except for these days of torrential rains.

He claimed homelessness with a broad grin
but he may have been a modest worker
in the nearby manufacture, perhaps in
a fast-food joint, for he wore their colors.

Well-spoken between a few stolen teeth
he seemed to know his theme
so close to nature as he was in the night
a happy man with something to share.

The Last Siren

Shrieking to the sleeper's tympanum
the dog howls in unison with
the last siren of the night somewhere
south of 2 am.

It follows the furious roar of the freight train
all the way to another catastrophe
of mangled rails tainted with a strange
paint like crimson asphalt.

The dog whimpers for a moment
it looks to the left, the right, attempts
to detect the scent of a life hanging
there, between ground and heavens.

Ambulances, fire Marshalls, and sheriffs,
they form a crowd about the scene
too late to release a breath into the
characters of the newest tragedies.

'Tis the way we live by the tolling bells
going through doors to eternity
perhaps the canine knows something
about the numbered days of his human pal.

But the body sleeps in the midst of the common din
dreaming of handsome landscapes far away
he may hope for the rescue the flashing lights
blue and red will undoubtedly provide him.

The Suicide Kid

The pain lingers awfully;
it may have been years
the basketball hoop still
stands, its net a little worn.

Parked before the house
his red truck remains;
father drives it from time to time
unable to part from it yet.

There are no more Christmases
too few joyful moments for
the aging parents as they recall
a teen boy with a broken heart.

They seem like strangers as
they ignore the neighbors who
drive near and attempt a sign
to let them know they are loved.

All they have now is the suffering
and a few moments with a yapping
puppy, as they recall the fateful day
the loud bang in their son's bedroom.

They Rush

They rush now,
they rush again in the morrow
they rush, rush, rush.

My strangers
wrapped in the loins of their exoskeletons
in multicolored hues bland as the street of Hades
from the heavens, they dive into the unknown
they ignore the warning of reckless speeds.

My acquaintances
standing tall above the rest as if on stilts
boasting treasures of arrogance and pride
accelerate through the mazes of their lives
they forget the beauty every turn may hide.

My foes
crawl near the meadows of dust
slithering between razor-sharp rocks
they hiss through the air with icy breaths
they never knew the gentleness of leisure.

My friends
quietly sitting on a swinging bench in early light
contemplating the unmoving scene before them
they live in the universal peace placed within;
they see their souls swell to magnificence.

They sleep
they sleep now,
they will sleep again in the morrow
they sleep, sleep, sleep.

Three Months Among Giants

Summer comes fast when at college
from a land far away in search of shelter
a little undergraduate in awe
sharing rent with the giants.

Tall, thin intellectuals wearing spectacles
barricaded behind columns of books to the ceiling
of a Victorian home property of the infamous
landlord amassing fortunes for lack of repair.

Brilliant in their studies of the Greeks
knowing all about Byron, Faulkner, and Kirkegaard
they quietly prepare for bashes of other types
unknown to the temporary tenant.

He contemplates them from his minuscule abode
these students on their way to the Ivies
as they speak a language made of puzzles
only their many all-nighters can justify.

To the little boy, they are geniuses
though he too peeks into the great classics
he is humbled by the likes of C. S. Lewis
discussing eternal life around a ½ keg of Guinness.

To the Master

He may have been as old as the stories he told
of faithful dogs in shining armor, with their
knights' adventures never completed.

They all wore magical rings
traveled alongside the likes of Aslan
fighting for the faint heart of many a lady.

We sat in the old house at the round table
smiling as he remained unaware of the joke
a few days before Christmas.

The tradition demanded wine and cheese
on the last evening of another term
so we honored the feast as he told his passionate tale.

Perhaps we remember little of those days
except for the heavy flakes outside
and our tipsy minds on our way home.

The dear old squire passed just a little later
but the images of those singular hours
will never recede to eternal oblivion.

To the Stronger Man

Mud fights in the desert
arm wrestling in a dream,
vain attempt at another marathon
swimming through the wide blue.

Satisfaction in your soul
you win again at the battle
of muscles and speed,
you, silly little brain.

Karma works its sly way through;
still taller you observed, than you,
a crime perhaps in your eerie realm;
what am I to do with those three inches?

Remember the old saying,
you can't win 'em all they say;
perhaps you can't win any at all
what will your epitaph say?

Little it took to shatter your world
but a perfect score in theory
an accident possibly in statistical studies
to you, self-humiliation.

So you are stronger;
take that to the grave old friend,
those who care are few and matter little
in this fleeting existence of the bones.

Touching the Truth

Darkness prevailed upon the eye of the weary;
another dawn turned to dusk in the early hours
amidst sounds numbed by a thickening mist.

A blazing light unseen atop the peaks
struck with the gentleness of a nurturing sun
gift to the one on a path to his eternal journey.

The senses of the body dissipated in a shell
carapace like a citadel to shelter a strange machinery
made to repeat the old chain of sufferance.

He is at last in a multitude he cannot fathom
as if suddenly an infinity of particles
everywhere at once in a same instant.

In waves, and strings, and wondrous corridors
every brush at the warm speed in flight is
one more glimpse within all truths revealed.

Unaware of what he used to be
outside of that thing called time
he knows without a doubt.

No mystery subsists in purpose
he can continue on forever
owner of the infinite destiny gifted him.

Truly

I have walked thousands of miles
around your aura.
never tiring of the automated motion;
I may wear limbs to mere memories.

Led by the great power of the
divine omniscience.
I will keep on the path to
the end times.

Taught by the omnipotent infinity
I will shed this flesh to release
the love God has for you.

Humbled by the glory of your being
my body longs to sublime;
you may be divinity incarnate,
unsuspecting
of your highest purpose.

Thus, looking to unfathomable horizons
I will never fear another step forward;
you are the end of the journey
where my soul has found eternal rest.

Visitor

She came rapping at my door
again; softly as to not awaken
the dreamer.

It seems it has become a custom
of hers; when I wonder whether she
will wander into my soul.

Not content with a single visit she
appeared twice more; perhaps she had
forgotten her purpose.

Carrying with her the gentleness of a fancy;
she seemed to float in a dress made of
summer and sun.

Giver of kisses and tender embraces she
is nothing but the home to long for from
the daily storms.

Always unexpected she comes too, seeking
a palace where she can rest; welcome among
all others.

You Make a Dream

You speak of Eustace with the passion of a little girl
Lucy, Suzanne, and those two princely boys.

Clive is a best friend across the ages
a man you met only in his words.

Another dreams when you speak the pearly sounds
holding your neck in a gentle tilt.

Sentences flow to the love of a father
caring thoughts for an aging mother.

Jealous for the air that envelopes you
he wants to walk in unison with your silhouette.

An invisible energy of infinite threads pulls him
so he may vanish in the universe of your being.

A world only of ideals swimming in your thoughts
deep intellect and wondrous emotions.

Her presence is a glorious palace made of divinity
where the hopeful child will always find rest.

You Who Love Me

I am thirty and so elegant
in memories I cannot erase
you walk the earth like a model
and I wonder what you see in me.

A photograph popped on social media
taken by a stranger in a strange locale
of a man I could barely recognize
not the one I see in the mirror.

When you smile, I dream
a word of you, a mere hello
I find heaven bound wings
perhaps you care that I live or die.

To be your friend such a gift
then your eyes smile with a kindness
greater with the passive days
it seems I mean more to you today.

What is it then. I ask, though I wish
in this skin sadly older than it thinks
as you stand with ageless beauty
the delicate whiteness of your hands.

What goes on in your heart I fathom
as you say little with your words
but write so much with your pen
just a little closer in the morrow, I guess.

And She Dances

Touch soft like the sweet breeze of early dawn,
her hand, so many droplets of a thin mist,
caresses the haze hovering over the land;
in the distance, sunny hues create a landscape.

In the stillness of all sounds she breathes in
a song to the ears of nature in subtle perfume,
swimming among the threads of her seemingly
celestial gown, glowing with a passion for being.

So light she seems to be floating through the days,
her face lighting each hour with diamond smiles,
on tiptoes of a ballerina she takes another step,
weightless as she brushes by.

She writes in the air with an invisible quill,
her hair undulating to the rhythm of her words,
smooth, a melody to times irremediable,
she carves every beat of her heart in eternity.

Her peaceful gaze nurtures all that surrounds her,
shining with the glory flowing through her veins,
life in her, so priceless, to be held dear and close;
a being, light, abundant, mysterious, ethereal.

Afraid of the Ghost

I awoke to the same image
a barren world painted in a rush
by strangers seeking a fleeting reward.

Heaven covered in a man-made lacquer
safe from rains and from snows
yet so hostile in its sterility.

The vision of tranquility ended
in the warm embrace
of a blessed night.

A sacred fancy made real by the dream
vanished in the dense air of dawn
fear swallowed my peace.

Too soon I was to encounter the ghost
made heavy with statuesque flesh
replica of such welcome apparition.

We would pass lives with a mere glance
a polite greeting perhaps a grin
to fill the veins with icy crystals.

Longing for bright darkness
I continued to rush through frozen hours
to be so reunited with the constancy of my infinite.

The Artist

Today the eminent surgeon wears a tuxedo
to penetrate the night adorned with roses
red as the nectar of steel he often scents.

Slender, he walks in a half confident step
his goal is the many marvels of another life
armed with the sharp blade, he aims to conquer.

His hands tremble as he contemplates the body
untamed, fertile, protected by the tallest fortress;
will the thin leaf cut through the leather of the armor?

It is as a terrible illness incurable, for fear of an end
worse yet than others experienced much too young
but to free her is the desire of one incomplete.

Within the heart of this soul, treasures endless lay
untouched, pure, perfect in their childish flesh
they deserve freedom beyond these glacial walls.

Leaning to the sleeping one, uneasy he acts as he must
cutting into the many stars as electricity passes through
she moves ever so slightly awakening from the deep.

No harm occurs, he continues the precise incision
slowly disappearing within a new world so desired
in this odd embrace of a most delicate passion.

Dear Mr. Biker

You did need to rev your engine against my eardrum,
the humming of my hybrid was like a soporific to my brain.

Mozart's concerto was playing, too melodious
on my satellite radio and fancy speakers.

Upward of ninety Fahrenheit in your world
I inhaled air online, refrigerated to sixty-eight.

You looked real cool with your Scottish cap
a roll of nicotine infused grass dangling from you blue lips.

You stared at me in my odorless world
and I think you laughed since you stink of gas.

Picture perfect of a living skeleton on a fiery horse to hell
your skin like a velum, colorful with images of nude ladies.

What a charmer you must be at the truck stop
when you mingle with those you envy at the wheel of their Macks.

I wonder whether that can of a cheap brew was still refreshing
when you disappeared in your shack of kids screaming.

Were you rushing to the glass pipe again
while watching reruns of WWF tournaments?

I cannot imagine brighter tales than this
with your Popeye face and fleshless frame.

Poor Child

I touch your hand with a shiver
so thin today in the wake of a loss.

No smiles in the world, no laughter
can hide the dark aura floating above.

The gentle glow of your usual joy
subdued by the weight of frigid dawns.

Your body with the grace of your soul
seems ghostly beneath the heavy chagrin.

I see the girl who skipped stones hours ago
and I seek the source of my inspiration.

Bathed in sacred tears you might sleep
so soft your fibers you may break.

I want to take another step forward
enter the distress, now your prisoner.

Behind the curtain of such great sorrow
you stand alone, crushed child.

Perhaps you will invite me for an embrace
so we may share the ice and the heat of hope.

For I need to break the ugly charm
that now shrouds you in the penumbra.

She, the Palimpsest

It is a holiday of sorts, a birthday, Valentine's day
in the midst of a scorching August
opening the secrets wrapped in mystery
a frenzied moment filled with hopes.

A chest revealed, safe with the unbreakable locks
another challenge to the trembling heart
of the adventurer in the quest for treasure
picturing previous stones within these walls.

Finding a box of black armor safe inside
he dares not reach to the traitorous hinges
fearing one more trick of the ignoble jokester
eyes closed, soul tense as steel, his fingers plunge.

Ruby walls of soft velvet comfort the weary touch
with a deep breath he accepts vulnerability
for the hour as he may discover still the unknown,
hidden by the illusory tenderness of a wish.

A concrete image comes to shape the exhausted mind
like the promise of a life cradled in a case made for eternity
diminutive it prolongs the nightmarish dream
into yet another world, cold as ice on satin, a stone lies.

Like the idol he sought, holding onto the light
blinded, he stares to the depth of the glassy rock
only to find behind the unbreakable skin, another
unattainable present to the next holiday, tomorrow perhaps.

Caldera

It is a beautiful thing to picture
images of the ideal in one's mind
alone surrounded by a quiet land.

I recall the heights of the caldera
bobcats ventured to dialogue with me
in the perfect silence of higher elevations.

Only breath and a few heartbeats
came to my ears as I scanned the horizon
a faint breeze caressing my cheeks.

What a privilege it is without distractions
to draw the perfect contours of the soul
as I stand in the immensity of the universe.

A memory of ten to twenty years
I keep with me as an eternal treasure
though you may be so near for me to touch you.

Around the World

I have been on a solo flight
far too long
at the helm of a soft glider
always a little closer
to a place that belongs to you.

Now the time has come
to approach the rich clearing
between the fruitful branches
of a most luscious orchard
find rest by your quiet stream.

There is no need for a ship now
or of parachute as
this body may gently slide
within the bank of an inviting flow
warm and soothing with love.

The journey ends in you
a spirit softly dozing upon yours
wake, sleep, or death all the same
the forest closes to the light of day
in each other's embrace forevermore.

Babe in the Rubble

She heard a groan
it came from far away
another hemisphere flying
above peaks and abysses.

She saw images of red and gray
tears made of soot in the somber hour
many fell to their knees in front of the giant
pleading and asking the eternal question.

She raced to the site of millennia
seeking entry upon the burning rubble
to make an everlasting offering to
a world lost in eternal trivialities.

Standing upon the mount of ruby red stones
still aflame from a strange origin and
a confusing destiny she brandished upward
the body of the babe who passed last eve.

She too shed a tear facing the revered idol
of darkened and charred oaken beams
and asked why the little one died with a million kin
but the waves keep silent and the mirrors hidden under a shroud.

Early Christmas Lights

It is never too soon in the day to wreck a life
"Sometimes, you just have to get someplace," they say
so what, if others get in the way!

6 AM on a Thursday morning, blue flashing lights
all across the four-lane highway and a cloud of steam
to give the scene an eerie aura.

6 and change a few days later, a mile sooner
a great red truck blocks the road to the office
another light ignored and a few more lives ruined.

Too soon to make that right turn, but you know
"if it's clear I'll go and give you hell with my horn,"
yet she promised not to move just to please your arrogance.

Daily ritual of our lives, I wonder what happened
in the centuries of horses and carriages
pedestrians holding their girls by the hand?

Garlands of blues and reds as the ambulance roars away
hoping the colors of the ICU will suffice to save the life
of the child caught watching toons in the Suburban.

That day I saw the flying doctors do their best as they rushed
her little body to the trauma center praying for another breath
only to make the front page in the next day's news.

There was also a photograph of the 49-year-old hurried man
leaning on the cruiser ready for his sentence
puzzled that he had done anything wrong.

The tears will never tarry when I ponder the fatal instant
a few drops of her sweet blood dripping from the helicopter
which I will not erase from the windshield of my Prius.

Grand New World

In their uniform gowns of pure snow they march on
the little girl caresses the smooth ramparts
of the only home she will ever know.

They are on the outing of their lives
family injected with perfect genes
without a worry, without a true purpose.

Trained to useless existences they might smile
if only a little pleasure was permitted within
but there are rules for those who want to survive

Their eyes are clear as if those of albinos
heads clean shaven they ape a terrifying pantomime
alone in corridors of safety, their assigned world.

Perhaps they dream of a past they never knew
hidden from them to protect this semblance of a human race
yet they dare not speak a hint of those thoughts.

They continue on slowly as it is supposed ghosts might
others wait their turn to inherit this void
so pure they will never know suffering.

Getting Old

She stared into a worn-out mirror
familiar motion of early morning rises
seeking the imperfection born of the darkness.

Uncertain in the first hours of early frosts
she passed her personal inspection
with the gaze of an unmatched surgeon.

Robed in the purity of the soft cotton
she caresses the gentle envelope of the years
complete in the glee that life still loans.

Remembering birthdays of another century
she wonders at the purity of the white satin
where not a line yet has written a somber destiny.

The assurance of time has gone into another realm
where dimensions come together into space
and she smiles even when they call her granny.

Our Parents' Age

It was not so long ago that you showed me
so many mysteries in the eye of a child
you, my hero, great god of our precious land
when you taught me to ride, to drive
to do all these things in the dirt and the rust.

Scars persist in reminding me of the cuts
the bruises and anxious moments in pain
as others played on a faraway beach
or joined their summer friends at camp
and I cherish the times under thunderous skies.

The sight of you caring for your garden
thick fingers handling the rake and the shears
preparing as you spoke in secret, the evening feast
before you wrote study guides
my lessons for another day, a life to come.

You two sleep now with your family
comforted by a well-deserved peace
and I walk this world still without pain
your age at last, an adult in his prime
yet a child slowly reaching the golden years.

What a wonder to contemplate the moments
when you provided everything a life needed
to grow in your steps, the boy unaware that
all you did was a sacrifice of your youth
to solemnly offer it, untouched.

Late-Night Stroll

They waltz in the intimacy of the boulevard
busy with the late-night crowds.

Ignoring the would-be onlookers
they embrace in their secret privacy.

Her light summer dress of angelic white
the suit of his armored heart soon
dissipate in universal mist.

Their eager lips join to celebrate
another hour spent in abandonment
quiet they breathe imperceptibly.

Transported to an alcove white as clouds
they have forgotten what is not of them
to be the one they created in their daily dreams.

The artist will make a safe place for them
on his canvas but the viewer will never know
who they might be in this undefinable form.

Vanished into each other they now sleep
holding in pleasant confusion what was once
the private land of the other.

Reservations Made

No need for a passport or ID
for the longest journey to unknown
places hidden from everyone's sight.

A simple seal upon a dubious diploma
sign that all things are to be put to smoke
scattered to winds on a greasy highway.

A signature crafted by a steady hand
'neath the cybernetic words of a machine
devoid of heart, yet so terminal.

Possessions shared, albeit so few
to those who never knew what pain
was the constant lot of the departed.

Merely vanished he will leave not a trace
upon the ground he hoped would welcome him
to gift his days with what many before were bequeathed.

The time has come to embark at last
on the journey to freedom from the shackles
of a life full of loveless abysses.

In the morrow, no one will notice that
a voice has been silenced, the air no longer moves
where once, he longed so much for her to come along.

Shroud of Pain

In the bright evening sun
a young dusk set upon a joyful day
for miles into a distant horizon.

But the night is not afraid of the light
in a heart yet so fragile for this life
it knows how to settle in frigid ice.

Alone behind the door, she awaited the news
anchored onto hope for a little longer
hours to change, to months perhaps.

Yet the shroud fell upon her lips
drowned in a sudden shower of sorrows
a flash of darkness under clear skies.

She fell to her knees before a stranger
alone with the grief so suddenly gifted her
the phone still crying in her weakened grip.

Pleading with those deep blues she asked
why he too must follow the herds
on such a glorious eve to join eternal sleeps.

Southern Rains

Balmy drops from heaven vanish upon a crash
infinite in their power to continue to no end
they make a wall to a transparent fortress.

The child escapes in her summer suit
to drink the essence of a world she cannot fathom
soon lost in a waltz with the realm which made her.

She slips on the slide of a wet grassy slope
but she will not fall until her dance is done
her pearly flesh shielded by the puerile waters.

Her lips laugh in the enjoyment of this great meal
as she swallows pieces of the universe
so much like her, full of the original burst.

Now the time has come to embrace her dream
dizzy with the swirls of her giddiness she abandons herself
under the delighted eye of so many caring souls.

Throne

The great king left a mark upon the oak
when he sat with Louis in the shade
of peace for a modern revolutionary.

The little man with the cross dreamed of gold
in a palace ornate with DaVinci and Vincent
stolen from his conquests at the point of a tank.

Arthur never reached his grail in the mist,
precious stones encrusted to the throne
the envy of tyrannic souls everywhere.

Nothing but a chair adorned with a title
pricey cloth and antlers of a murdered elk
for centuries to ponder the greatness of another corpse.

The Kid's Alright

Those feet may weigh a thousand pounds
as they pummel the back of the theater bench

No more than four feet from the dirt
a little devil fights the jitters.

Two giants stand by pretending
they see, hear, feel nothing.

The old man trembles with anxiety
glued to a place he never wanted.

Dreaming of an old-time spanking
he grinds his teeth to bear the moment.

Alone with the playbill, he recalls
days familiar as yesterday's.

When he felt no concern for those who,
like him, now grew a little impatient.

He takes a deep breath now and realizes
the kid's okay after all.

The Sweet Smell of Science

Graying hair in tangle-like spider webs perhaps
a view onto the meandering mind constant
in its infinite bewilderment.

Hunched above the blueish flames
an aging nose drowned in mysterious fumaroles
he might be of bronze at his centennial desk.

Darkness has long mastered the day's light
silence permeates the walls of unperturbed corridors
the steps of many curious onlookers no longer echo.

Relic, armed with an arsenal of inquisitive tools
his life seems frozen in the never-land of his queries
heavy eyelids refuse to shut for fear of a miss.

It might be formaldehyde or a deadly venom
the scent which arises surrounding the ghost
discoverer of tickling secrets.

We will leave him for now to his own
strange creature forgotten behind colorful potions
so he may contemplate the formulas as we may love letters.

Living at 55

It is all a matter of time
as he watches from the windows
darkened by years of abandon
an old cinemascope movie at twenty-four frames per second
a super high definition at twenty-nine
lives moving by at fifty-five.

They come and they go without a sign
making not a trace upon the present
no memory of their passage remains for the future
no story to be told for these unknown ghosts
in a rush to reach the next stop sign
another supper with friends becoming strangers.

They hit the asphalt in the early hours
to slide by again as the skies darken
hoping for a smooth journey to their temporary homes
while some will crash into an unseen oblivion
remembered for a few lines in the morning news
most will merely perish asleep at high speed.

Fixated on the lights ahead, their dreams too are in slumber
fleshy robots they no longer ask those puerile questions
of those years when still attempting to survive
their souls have been subdued by the unavoidable race
intoxicated by the unbearable sleeping agent they call a life
they continue on the path unable to rediscover their extinct
fancies.

Travelers

It is nine past yesterday again
and they wait glaring at the screen
behind the glass where the animals land.

Twenty-seven snacks ago there were five
now their number staggers to the undefined,
surrounded by crackling cellophane.

One yawns to deep displeasure;
behind their fortress uniforms glitter without a care
it will be six past another week soon enough.

Prisoners of this jungle they know so well
they sit, they lay, they stand, they strike up words
with oddities not unlike them yet never before seen.

Behind their citadel three laugh to a story only they know
watching over the cattle they feed to keep in silence
all is illusion of motion in this world of melting wax.

The seconds sit on a frozen clock, giggling in secret
the cackling continues between resigned creatures
It is three past today, and nothing has changed.

Wine Tasting, Cottonwood, Az, June 2023

You may remind me
kindly as I know you will
that I too am collecting the years
but I too will underscore a detail
that I do not own a mirror to tell the truth.

To be honest, you have to admit that
I am the only one of my kind
wearing breeches and a would-be cowboy hat
far away from my ranch in the hills
of my sweet home in Appalachia.

This is the valley of hottest climes
surrounded by deserts, a gentle oasis
for retirees seeking to expand
the energy so long chained up
in manicured lives of unreal cities.

I recall my pals in Paris when they too
enjoyed a meal made of unspoken pleasures
while lives passed them by in so much hurry
but not here, for you see, time has stopped
within vortexes mysterious as their first settlers.

What You Left Behind

I watch the garden change my mother
where the earth has been turned many times since
you walked away from your beloved fields
a world you could enter with unending grace.

Into the barn it seems every corner recalls
the sound of the hammer and the saw
as you built my father another shed to
those beasts you cared for like no other.

Near the hearth I recall the fragrance
of those meals you imagined for my childhood
granny as you aged in timeless decades
your braided hair often wild as a teen's.

I seek you in every room dear siblings
when you return to your home so far away
to find but a few lines in the dust of my road
abandoned rappers of a sweet delight.

Your lives are saved in layers of time
like coats of paint in an ageless palimpsest
a quilt visible only to those who knew you,
with every piece a jolt to a slowing heart.

When I Hear the Ninth

I have taken ten million steps through a wilderness
in the savage land of a city I know too well
listening to the notes Wolfgang left behind.

The playful rascal waltzes in my brain
as I fly through the rugged land of my backyard.
I hear him giggle impressed by the wit of his own obscenities.

He lives near Ludwig, Frederick, and Arthur
surrounded by Salvador, Claude, and Mary
all rejoicing in the paradise they were gifted.

There too I find a simple father smiling
who never had a moment for the arts
blossoming in a world his for all time.

I see Amadeus, his wand in hand
dying of a rapid youth, his soul afire
alive in every bar with every stroke.

Heaven in my head dances with eternal minds
Mozart full of joy will never die
as he awards the mayhem of his existence to all.